Elsa
the Mistletoe
Fairy

Join the **Rainbow Magic Reading Challenge!**

Read the story and collect your fairy points to climb the
~~Reading Rainbow at the back of the book.~~

Wishing Lara and Isla a magical Christmas x

Special thanks to
Rachel Elliot

ORCHARD BOOKS

First published in Great Britain in 2016 by The Watts Publishing Group

1 3 5 7 9 10 8 6 4 2

© 2016 Rainbow Magic Limited.
© 2016 HIT Entertainment Limited.
Illustrations © Orchard Books 2016

HiT entertainment

A CIP catalogue record for this book is available from the British Library.

ISBN 978 1 40834 264 0

Printed and bound in Great Britain by CPI Group (UK) Ltd, Croydon, CR0 4YY

MIX
Paper from
responsible sources
FSC® C104740

FSC
www.fsc.org

The paper and board used in this book are made from wood from responsible sources

Orchard Books
An imprint of Hachette Children's Group
Part of The Watts Publishing Group Limited
Carmelite House, 50 Victoria Embankment, London EC4Y 0DZ

An Hachette UK Company
www.hachette.co.uk
www.hachettechildrens.co.uk

Elsa
the Mistletoe
Fairy

by Daisy Meadows

ORCHARD

www.rainbowmagic.co.uk

The Fairyland Palace

Hilltop

Sledging Hill

Wetherbury Village

Christmas Market

Kirsty's House

Jack Frost's Spell

Goblins, stop snoring and get out of bed!
The Royal Christmas Gala must not go ahead.
I can't stand this jollity one second more.
So I'll steal Elsa's things and cause sorrow galore.

The fairies want dancing and music and food,
But I will make sure that I dampen their mood.
The thought of those pests having fun makes me mad.
So let's mess up their plans, and let's see them all sad!

The Goodwill Lip Balm

Contents

Winter in Wetherbury

"Wheeeeee!"

Kirsty Tate and Rachel Walker zoomed down the snowy hill on a sledge, cosily wrapped up in their warmest clothes. All they could hear was the swish-swoosh of the sledge on the crisp snow. They squealed with laughter as the sledge plunged into a snowdrift at the bottom of the hill, and they tumbled into the soft whiteness.

Giggling and rosy-cheeked, the best friends helped each other up and brushed the snow from their winter coats. Their breath puffed into the air like smoke. Ahead of them, the roofs of Wetherbury village were heavy with snow.

"We have to leave the sledge here for the next person to pull back up the hill," said Kirsty. "While the roads are all covered in snow, it's the quickest way around the village."

"It's so quiet and beautiful," said Rachel. "I like it this way."

"Me too," Kirsty agreed. "This is going to be one of the most Christmassy Christmases ever."

Instead of cars roaring along the streets, children were out building snowmen in the middle of the road. Grown-ups and children were whizzing down the hills on shared sledges instead of walking, and everyone was taking their turn to pull the sledges back to the tops of the hills.

"I'm so happy you're staying with us while the Wetherbury Christmas Market is running," Kirsty said as they scrunched their way towards the village centre. "It's on for three days – today, Saturday and Sunday – and it's so magical."

"Then I'm sure I'm going to love it," said Rachel, with a smile. "Magic seems to follow us around, doesn't it?"

Kirsty smiled too. Together, they had shared many secret adventures with their fairy friends, and they knew the tingling excitement of magic in the air. Just then, thick flakes of snow began to fall again, and the girls tucked their scarves around them even more tightly.

"If the snow keeps falling at this rate I won't just be here for three days," said Rachel. "I might be spending the whole of Christmas in Wetherbury!"

Kirsty looked up at the falling snowflakes and grinned.

"Keep falling!" she shouted, throwing out her arms and twirling around. "I want my best friend to stay with me for ever!"

When they arrived in the middle of the village, it was already bustling with people. A red banner was hanging above the main street, covered with golden writing.

Welcome to Wetherbury Christmas Market!

Friday: Christmas decorations for home and tree
Saturday: Christmas food
Sunday: Christmas presents, cards and wrapping paper

Merry Christmas, everyone!

15

Below the banner, little stalls lined the
street, sparkling with tinsel, coloured glass
and sequinned decorations. The air was
filled with the scents of cinnamon, roasted
chestnuts and steaming hot chocolate.
Rachel and Kirsty strolled from stall to
stall, picking up delicate hand-painted

glass baubles, thick garlands of tinsel and shiny holly wreaths.

"Everything looks and smells so good," said Rachel, pausing beside the roasted-chestnut stall. "Shall we share a bag of these?"

A few minutes
later the girls
were standing
beside the
mistletoe stall,
their mittened
hands around
warm paper bags
full of chestnuts.

"These are
delicious," said
Kirsty, before
popping another chestnut into her mouth.
"I wish it could be Christmas all year
round!"

They slipped down the side of the
mistletoe stall, sheltering from the flurries
of snow in the narrow space between
stalls. Kirsty glanced up and saw a few

sprigs of mistletoe hanging down above them.

"The berries are almost as white as snow," she said. "Oh my goodness – one of them is glowing!"

Rachel and Kirsty gazed up at the single, shining mistletoe berry, and then looked at each other.

"Magic!" they said together.

A Festive Invitation

The people walking along the street were browsing the stalls or keeping their heads down against the snow. None of them was looking down the narrow gap where the girls were standing. Rachel and Kirsty looked up again. The bright berry was swelling, just like a balloon being blown up. It grew bigger and bigger

until … POP! It burst with a
jingling of tiny
bells, and a
little fairy was
fluttering in its
place.

"Hello!" said
the fairy in a
bright voice. "I'm
Elsa the Mistletoe
Fairy."

Her dress was the
colour of a mistletoe
berry, and her shoes glittered like
snow in the sunshine. She shook back her
golden hair and smiled at the girls.

"It's lovely to meet you," said Rachel.
"You must be one of the fairies that looks
after Christmas."

Elsa nodded. "It's my job to make sure that every Christmas is better than the one before," she said. "We want everyone's year to end happily – especially yours! I've come to invite you both to King Oberon and Queen Titania's Royal Christmas Gala as the guests of honour. It's on Sunday in Fairyland – will you come?"

She gazed at them with eager eyes, and the girls clasped each other' hands in excitement.

"Guests of honour?" Kirsty repeated. "We'd love to come – but why us?"

"Because you have helped Fairyland so many times," said Elsa, opening her arms. "As soon as the king and queen asked me to organise the gala, I thought of you. They were delighted to agree."

"Thank you so much!" said Rachel. "Shall we use our lockets to travel to the Fairyland Palace?"

Queen Titania had given each of them a locket containing enough  fairy dust to bring them to Fairyland. But Elsa shook her head.

"You will be magically brought to Fairyland at seven o'clock on Sunday evening," she said.

"I can hardly wait!" said Kirsty.

"I *can't* wait," said Rachel, hopping from one foot to the other.

Elsa laughed. "Would you like to come now and help with the preparations?" she asked.

The girls hugged each other, jumped and down, squealed and then hugged again.

"I think that's a yes!" said Elsa.

She glanced around to check that no one was watching, and then waved her wand. A thin, silvery ribbon whirled around the girls and whisked them into the air beside Elsa, shrinking them to fairy size. Wings as delicate as snowflakes unfolded on their backs, and a sprig of mistletoe floated down from the stall to hover between them. Elsa's wand danced above it, coiling it into the shape of a carriage with mistletoe-berry wheels and mistletoe-leaf seats.

The snow was falling even more thickly now, hiding them from the sight of any curious human eyes. Elsa tapped one of the carriage doors with her wand, and it opened at once.

"Please, climb in," she said.

The leaf seats were soft and springy, and changed to fit their shape when they sat down. As soon as they were ready, the carriage lifted them high into the winter sky and whisked them away. They tried to look out of the window, but all they could see were the swirling flakes of snow. Then there was a change in the light outside, the carriage sank downwards, and the door flew open. They had arrived at the Fairyland Palace.

Sudden Squabbles

"Welcome!" called a friendly voice.

Rachel and Kirsty stepped out of the carriage and saw Bertram the frog footman smiling at them from the doorway of the palace.

"Hello, Bertram!" called Rachel. "How are you?"

"All the better for seeing you," Bertram replied with a bow.

"The gala is being held in the
ballroom," said Elsa, linking her arms
through theirs. "Let's go and see how the
decorating is going!"

Rachel and Kirsty paused in the
doorway of the ballroom, smiling. Their
friends the Showtime Fairies were
fluttering around the room, draping

garlands of holly, tinsel and mistletoe
from corner to corner and against the
walls. Silver trays were floating from fairy
to fairy, carrying goblets of delicious-
smelling drinks and snowman- and
reindeer-shaped gingerbread. The merry
chatter and laughter of the fairies made
the room seem twice as full.

"Rachel! Kirsty!" cried Leah the
Theatre Fairy, spotting them.

The seven fairies zoomed towards them
and pulled them into a big hug.

"We're here to help Elsa prepare for the
gala," said Darcey the Dance Diva Fairy.
"We didn't know that you'd be here.
What a lovely surprise!"

"It's a lovely surprise for us, too,"

said Kirsty, gazing up at the fancy decorations. "It looks as if the gala is going to be a spectacular event!"

"There will be special performances and lots of dancing," said Elsa. "Even Jack Frost is here to watch the preparations and enjoy a Christmassy glass of mulled blackcurrant cordial."

To their surprise, the girls saw that Jack Frost was indeed sitting on a golden chair in the corner. His cloak was wrapped tightly around him, and his spiky head was bowed over a plate of gingerbread.

33

"It's not like him to be so quiet," Rachel whispered to Kirsty as the Showtime Fairies flew off to carry on with the decorating.

"I can't see his face, but I bet he's looking grumpy," Kirsty whispered back. "He never likes to see the fairies having fun."

Just then, they heard raised voices from the other side of the ballroom.

"Red!" Taylor the Talent Show Fairy snapped at Madison the Magic Show Fairy.

"It has to be *red!*"

"*Silver* tinsel would look much prettier on the tables," Madison argued, her hands on her hips. "Don't you have any taste?"

Leah pulled a foil chain down from the ceiling, frowning at Darcey.

"You've hung it all wrong!" she complained.

Suddenly the whole ballroom was filled with the sound of bickering fairies.

Rachel, Kirsty and Elsa stared at the
Showtime Fairies.

"What is wrong with everyone?" Elsa
asked in confusion.

There was a commotion in the hall
outside the ballroom, and then Holly
the Christmas Fairy
zoomed in and
darted to Elsa's
side, taking her
hand.

"Elsa, I'm
afraid I've got
some bad news,"
she said. "There's
been a robbery in
Holly Berry Lane. All three of your
magical objects have been stolen!"

Looking horrified, Elsa sank into a

nearby chair. Rachel and Kirsty stared at Holly in shock.

"What's Holly Berry Lane?" Kirsty asked.

"It's the home of all the fairies who help look after Christmas," Holly explained. "Elsa, I'm sure that Rachel and Kirsty will have an idea that will help."

But Elsa didn't seem to be listening. She was staring into space.

"How am I going to organise the Christmas Gala?" she asked. "How can I keep everyone happy in the human world without my magical objects?"

Rachel put her arm around Elsa's shoulders.

"Tell us about your magical objects," she said in a gentle voice.

37

"The goodwill lip balm is filled with Christmas spirit that helps everyone get on well with each other at Christmas," Elsa explained in a flat  voice. "The precious pudding makes sure that all Christmas food tastes delicious, and the inviting invitation ensures that everyone gets to their Christmas parties safely and on time."

"So that's why everyone is arguing all of a sudden," said Rachel. "Without the goodwill lip balm, they have no Christmas spirit and they all just feel irritable and cross."

"This is the kind of thing Jack Frost would do," said Kirsty. "But it can't be him this time – he hasn't left our sight."

"You're right, he's been here all morning," said Elsa.

"Maybe it was his goblins?" Holly suggested.

"They're not organised enough to do a robbery by themselves," said Kirsty. "Who else could it be?"

"I don't know anyone else who would do something so mean," said Elsa, raking her fingers through her hair.

"We *could* ask the Barn Elf," said Kirsty. "We met him when we were helping Robyn the Christmas Party Fairy. He isn't loyal to the fairies or to Jack Frost, but he might know something about what's happened."

"He might even be playing a trick himself," said Rachel, remembering the mischievous elf who lived in the middle of a distant forest.

Elsa rose to her feet, looking calm and determined.

"It's the best idea we have at the moment," she said. "Will you come with me, Rachel and Kirsty?"

"Of course," Rachel replied, as they stepped forward to stand on either side of her. "Wherever you go, we'll be right by your side."

Tricks and Disguises

Rachel glanced across at Jack Frost as they headed out of the ballroom, and saw that his shoulders were shaking. As they reached the ballroom door, she stopped.

"Just a minute," she said, thinking hard. "I've suddenly got a funny feeling that we're being tricked."

She turned and zoomed over to Jack
Frost's side. He was still bent over the
gingerbread and she couldn't see his face.

"Merry Christmas, Jack Frost," she said.

There was no reply, so she said it again.
Jack Frost coughed.

"Merry Christmas," he squawked.

"That's not Jack
Frost's voice!"
Rachel exclaimed.

She pulled
off his cloak
and saw
two goblins,
one sitting
on the
shoulders
of the
other.

"Ha ha!" the goblins cried, leaping to
their feet. "Jack Frost has tricked all you
stupid fairies!"

They knocked over the blackcurrant
cordial, crammed more gingerbread
biscuits into their mouths and ran out
of the ballroom. Rachel, Kirsty and Elsa
stared at each other.

"It's starting to make sense," said Kirsty. "Of course Jack Frost is the thief! He sent his goblins to the ballroom so that we wouldn't suspect him."

"The goblins have gone to warn him," said Elsa. "We have to find him before he finds out that we've discovered his trick!"

"Let's fly to the Ice Castle," said Rachel. "We should be able to get there faster than the goblins."

They darted out of the palace and zoomed off in the direction of Jack Frost's frozen home. Soon they were hovering outside the castle door, trying to catch their breath.

"I don't think I've ever flown so fast," said Kirsty. "But how are we going to get in?"

"The goblins!" Rachel exclaimed. "Elsa,

can you make us look like the goblins
who tricked us at the palace? If Jack
Frost thinks that we are the ones who
helped his plan to work, he might let us
see the magical objects."

With a swift tap of Elsa's wand on
their heads, Rachel
and Kirsty felt their
noses growing,
their heads
swelling and
their feet
widening. In
a few seconds,
they were
exact copies of
the goblins from the
palace. Rachel even had the cloak they
had been wearing tucked under her arm.

"I'll hide in there,"
said Elsa, pointing
to the snowy
branches of a
nearby tree.
"Good luck, my
friends!"

Rachel and
Kirsty pushed
open the door and
marched into the castle. Their hearts
were pounding, but they knew that they
couldn't let Elsa down. They had been
inside Jack Frost's castle several times
before, and they knew the way to his
Throne Room. Soon they were standing
outside the half-open door.

"Well, come in then!" snarled Jack
Frost from inside. "Why are you dancing

around outside my door, jelly brains?"

The girls slipped in and saw Jack Frost sitting with one leg hooked over the arm of his throne. He was cackling to himself and holding a tiny, glittering jar between his thumb and forefinger.

"The goodwill lip balm!" Kirsty whispered. "That must be it!"

"What are you whispering about?" Jack Frost demanded. "Come here!"

The girls scurried forwards, and Jack Frost pulled out a small Christmas pudding and twirled it on the tip of his

finger. There was also a glowing piece of paper sticking out from beneath his cloak.

"The precious pudding and the inviting invitation!" Rachel said with a gasp.

The First Object

"Well?" Jack Frost demanded. "Were you discovered?"

The girls exchanged an anxious look.

"No one has discovered who we really are," said Kirsty truthfully.

"*Yet*," added Rachel under her breath.

Jack Frost cackled and rubbed his hands together with glee.

"I'm so clever!" he crowed. "I know you all want to be like me, but you could never be quick or clever or handsome or tall enough. Hah!"

"Please may we see the things you took?" Rachel asked. "After all, we were helpful."

Jack Frost let out a snort, but he tossed the little pot to her and she caught it.

"Mine will be the only Christmas party worth attending," he boasted. "The stupid fairies' Christmas Gala will be ruined!"

Kirsty and Rachel were barely listening to him.

"How are we going to get the other objects back?" Kirsty whispered.

Rachel was about to reply when the Throne Room door crashed open and the real goblins raced in, with Elsa flying close behind them.

"Impostors!" the goblins gabbled. "Fairy frauds! A horrible hoax!"

Jack Frost had gone purple with rage.

"Idiots!" he roared at the goblins. "Nincompoops! You got caught!"

"I'm sorry!" cried Elsa, transforming the girls back into fairies again. "I couldn't stop them!"

"Catch them!" Jack Frost screamed at the goblins.

But Elsa aimed her wand at one of the windows, and it sprang open for her. As Jack Frost leaped to catch them, they sped out through the window and zoomed back towards the palace.

"He's shaking his fist at us," said Rachel, looking back over her shoulder. "Probably because we got this!"

With a smile, she tossed the glittery little pot towards Elsa, who caught it and spun a pirouette in mid-air.

"I can't believe it!" she cried. "The goodwill lip balm!"

"I'm sorry we couldn't get the rest of

your magical objects," said Kirsty. "But
we *will* get them – very soon!"

"I think you're both amazing," said
Elsa, as they flew down to the palace.
"Thank you!"

"Jack Frost won't get his own way,"
Rachel said.

She led Elsa and Kirsty into the
ballroom, where the Showtime Fairies
were once again working happily
together on the gala preparations.

"You see?" said Rachel. "In the end,
friendship is stronger than anything Jack
Frost can do to upset us."

"You're both wonderful," said Elsa.
"May I call on your help again soon?
I have to find the other two magical
objects before the gala on Sunday."

"We'd love to help," said Kirsty at once.
"And we want to make
sure that the gala is
perfect for all our
fairy friends."

Elsa smiled,
and then with
a wave of her
wand, the girls
were back in
the middle of the
Christmas Market.

58

A few magical sparkles fell to the snowy ground and disappeared.

"What a wonderful start to your visit," said Kirsty, her eyes shining with excitement. "Adventure, magic and a Royal Gala. I can't wait to find out what's going to happen to us next!"

The Precious
Pudding

Contents

Mouldy Mince Pies

"What day is it today?" asked Mrs Tate, Kirsty's mother.

"Saturday," said Kirsty, laughing. "How could you forget that, Mum?"

Mrs Tate laughed too.

"It's because we're so snowed in here in Wetherbury," she said. "No one can get to work or do anything they usually do.

Every day feels like a Saturday to me!"

It was the second day of the Christmas Market, and they were strolling around the stalls together. The snow was only falling lightly, and there was even a patch of blue sky high above. Rachel and Kirsty exchanged happy smiles, their cheeks pink and their eyes sparkling.

"Roll up!" called a burly stallholder in a striped apron. "Today it's all about Christmas food! We've got everything you could wish for right here in Wetherbury. Sugared almonds, mince pies, clotted cream, pickles, crackers, cheese, cookies – don't walk by, come and try!"

His deep laugh rang around the crowded village street and made it seem more Christmassy than ever. The scents of oranges, pine leaves, cinnamon, coffee and roasted nuts mixed deliciously in the air.

"Handmade chocolates!" called a young woman at the next stall. "Violet creams and peppermint fondants! Raspberry swirls and nut truffles! Try before you buy!"

She held out a plate filled with
scrumptious-looking sweets, and the girls
picked one each, while Mrs Tate crossed
the street to try some mince pies.

"These look yummy," said Rachel.

Kirsty took a bite, and then pulled a
face.

"Ugh, this violet
cream tastes like
sawdust," she
said in a quiet
voice.

Rachel
nibbled her
sugar mouse
and then put
her hand to her
mouth.

"It's salty!" she whispered.

They moved away from the stall and dropped the sample sweets into a bin.

"The next stall has sweets too," said Kirsty. "Let's see if we can sample theirs instead."

But the next stall's candy canes were watery and soft.

"I don't think much of that stall over there," said Mrs Tate, hurrying to rejoin the girls. "Their mince pies tasted absolutely horrible!"

Rachel and Kirsty gazed around the market. Everywhere they looked, people were wincing and screwing up their mouths as they tasted the food on offer. Most of the stallholders were looking worried and upset.

"It's very strange," Mrs Tate went on. "Usually the food here is absolutely delicious. I can't understand it."

71

"I can," said Rachel in a low voice.

"Me too," said Kirsty. "The food tastes bad because Jack Frost has stolen Elsa's precious pudding."

Mrs Tate moved off to try the mince pies at a different stall. The girls were about to follow her when Rachel turned around and stared at a cake stall behind them.

"What's wrong?" asked Kirsty in surprise.

"I just saw someone disappearing around the back of that stall," Rachel whispered. "Someone *green!*"

"We have to find out if it was a goblin," said Kirsty. "Mum! We're just going to look at this cake stall!"

Mrs Tate nodded and waved, and the girls darted over to the cake stall. The sign above said 'Baker Jack's' and a lot of people had gathered in front of it.

"I can't see the cakes at all," said Rachel, jumping up and down at the back of the crowd. "I can't even see the stallholders."

Just then, a lady elbowed her way out through the crowd of shoppers.

"Their cakes are the best I have ever tasted," she said, her arms full of cake boxes. "And their pies are simply delicious!"

"Scrumptious!" a man shouted, cake crumbs flying from his mouth.

Kirsty started jumping up and down too.

"I think I saw a long, green nose," she said, panting. "Oh, Rachel, we have to get closer. What are we going to do?"

Worse Than Goblins!

"It must be the goblins," said Kirsty. "And I bet they have the precious pudding. They're selling the only tasty food on the whole market!"

The best friends stared at each other, trying to decide on a plan.

"Should we travel to Fairyland and fetch Elsa?" asked Rachel. "She could fly over the crowd and see what's going on."

"Let's try to find out for certain that it
is the goblins," said Kirsty. "If we can get
to the back of the stall, we might be able
to see what's going on inside. Then we
can use our lockets to travel to Fairyland
and tell Elsa what's happening."

Holding hands, the
girls crept down
the narrow
gap between
the stalls
and slipped
around to
the back.
The cake
stall was
covered in a
cheery red-and-
green cloth, but there was no entrance.

"How do we see anything if there's no way in?" Kirsty asked in a whisper.

"We'll have to lift the edge of the cloth and look underneath," said Rachel. "Fingers crossed it'll be OK. The stallholders will be busy serving the customers so they'll have their backs to us."

Rachel went first. Holding her breath, she slowly lifted the cloth that covered the stall and then froze.  Had anyone seen her? Had anyone heard her? No one shouted or came running, so she kept lifting the cloth until she was able to fit underneath.

Then she beckoned to Kirsty, who followed her under the cloth and into the stall.

Rachel and Kirsty crouched at the back of the stall. The noise from the customers was deafening. People were demanding cakes, biscuits and pies, and arguing with each other about who was next in the queue. There were two stallholders selling food, one tall and one short. They were standing on upturned wooden crates and each of them was wearing a Christmassy apron, tied with red ribbons. If they turned around, they would see the girls instantly.

Kirsty nudged Rachel and then pointed upwards.

"Look!" she mouthed.

There was a shelf above them on

the back wall of the stall. It was filled
with pies, buns, cakes and pastries. In
the centre was a very special-looking
pudding. It had a slight sparkle, and
when she looked at it, Rachel felt sure
that it didn't belong in the human world.

"Elsa's magical pudding," she said
under her breath. "We've found it!"

"Let's try to get it now," said Kirsty.
"We're so close!"

Rachel looked up at the stallholders. Their red apron ribbons were dancing in the frosty breeze, and this gave her an idea.

"If we tie the ribbons together, it might stop the goblins for long enough for us to grab the precious pudding and run," she said.

Keeping as low as they could, the girls tiptoed over to the first stallholder. His ribbon was tied in a big bow. Kirsty took one end and Rachel took the other. As slowly

as they could, they pulled the ends and
the ribbon loosened.

"So far, so good," said Kirsty in
Rachel's ear. "Now for the second
goblin!"

They crouched behind him and each
took one of the ribbon ends. But just as
they started to pull, he suddenly gave a
deafening yell.

"Come and get your Christmas goodies
at the only stall worth visiting!"

Rachel and Kirsty jumped, tugging on
the apron. The stallholder spun around
so fast his hat fell off. He glared down
at them, his eyes blazing. His spiky hair
was tipped with snow, and his beard was
bristling with anger. This wasn't a goblin.
It was Jack Frost himself!

Catering Confusion

Jack Frost bent down and grabbed both of the girls. His bony fingers dug into their shoulders like claws.

"I'll make you sneaky humans sorry for trespassing on *my* stall!" he snarled. "Robbers! Thieves!"

"We're not robbers or thieves," said Kirsty, trying to shake herself out of his grip. "All we want is to return the precious pudding to its rightful owner."

"*I'm* its rightful owner, you interfering little weed," Jack Frost retorted.

"Don't be so rude to my best friend," said Rachel. "Give the precious pudding back to Elsa and stop trying to spoil the Christmas Market – *and* the Fairyland Christmas Gala!"

"Bossy boots," said Jack Frost, sticking out his tongue at her.

"It's not bossy to know the right thing to do," said Rachel.

"Well, I know the right thing to do for *me*," said Jack Frost, "and that's all that counts. I'm going to make myself feel better by sending that stupid pudding somewhere truly GROTTY! You'll never find it!"

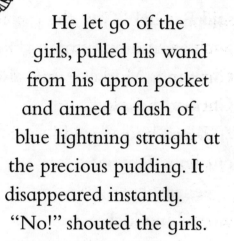

He let go of the
girls, pulled his wand
from his apron pocket
and aimed a flash of
blue lightning straight at
the precious pudding. It
disappeared instantly.

"No!" shouted the girls.

But cheers and applause from the
crowd deafened their cries.

"People think it's all part of the
Christmas Market fun," said Kirsty, giving
a groan. "Come on, Rachel, let's get out
of here."

They stumbled out of the stall with the cackles of Jack Frost ringing in their ears.

"We've made things worse," said Rachel, feeling guilty. "We have to find Elsa straight away and tell her what's happened."

"Let's go to Fairyland," said Kirsty, opening the locket that always hung around her neck.

There was no one in sight. Rachel opened her matching locket and held it up.

"On the count of three," she said. "One, two, three – please take us to Elsa!"

They blew their fairy dust over each other, and to their astonishment it turned into glittering snowflakes in mid-air. The magical snowflakes lifted them high above the Christmas Market and whisked them into a flurry of bigger snowflakes that were starting to fall on Wetherbury. The girls held tight to each other as they spun higher and higher, shrinking to fairy size. Their gauzy wings looked as white as the snow around them.

"I feel dizzy!"
Kirsty cried,
giggling as
she felt cold
snowflakes
landing on her
tongue.

"Close your
eyes!" Rachel called
out, squeezing her own eyes shut.

Kirsty closed her eyes too. After being
whirled around and hearing the wind
whoosh past their ears, the girls stopped
moving and felt solid ground beneath
their feet. They opened their eyes and
found themselves in an enormous kitchen.
Sunlight streamed through tall arch-
shaped windows, lighting up gleaming
surfaces and shining silver ovens. Lots of

fairies were fluttering back and forth in white chef's coats and hats, stirring bowls full of currant-cake mix and whipping egg whites into meringues. Rachel and Kirsty clapped their hands together in delight, but then they noticed that all the fairies looked unhappy, and there was a strong smell of burning in the air. Something was very wrong.

Elsa was standing by a table in the middle of the kitchen, her head in her hands. Rachel and Kirsty darted to her side.

"Are you all right?" Rachel asked.

Elsa looked at them and tried to smile.

"I'm glad to see you both," she said. "This is the first good thing that's happened all day!"

"What do you mean?" said Kirsty.

"The food for the gala is a disaster," said Elsa. "The egg whites won't stiffen, the cake mixtures are gritty, the cupcakes won't rise, the icing won't set and the gingerbread is as hard as rock. Everything the royal chefs have made tastes *horrible*, and it's my fault. I should never have let my magical objects out of my sight."

"You can't blame yourself for Jack Frost being mean and spiteful," said Kirsty.

"If you want to blame someone, blame us," Rachel added. "Because of us, the precious pudding might be lost for ever!"

A Journey Into Danger

The girls quickly told Elsa what had just happened in Wetherbury. She jumped up and hugged them.

"It's not your fault," she said. "We probably have a better chance of getting the pudding back now, because Jack Frost isn't guarding it. We just have to work out where he could have sent it."

Kirsty thought
hard, trying to
remember
everything
that Jack
Frost
had said.
Suddenly, an
idea struck
her.

"Jack Frost
told us that he was sending the precious
pudding somewhere truly *grotty*," she
said. "Those were his exact words. I
thought he was just being mean, but
what if he meant it? Do you think he
could have hidden the pudding in Goblin
Grotto?"

"The goblin village?" said Elsa, looking

alarmed. "It's possible – and it's the best clue we have right now. But I don't know if I feel brave enough to fly into the home of the goblins. I wouldn't know where to look."

"You don't have to do it alone," said Rachel. "We'll be right by your side, and we've been to Goblin Grotto before."

"With you two beside me, I feel brave enough to do anything!" Elsa exclaimed.

She used her magic to dress all three of them in warm coats, with big woolly hats that they could pull down low to disguise their faces. Then she waved her wand and the bright sunshine disappeared. Instantly, hail was hammering down on them and they were up to their ankles in grey slush. They had arrived in the centre of the goblin village.

All around them, goblins were hurrying along with their heads down against the hail and the freezing wind. Not one of them looked up at the fairies. Rachel smiled at Kirsty and Elsa.

"At least this bad weather means we can't be seen," she said. "I just wish the hail didn't sting quite so much!"

Elsa winked at her. Then she tapped
a lamppost at the corner of the street.
It sprang into the air, folded up like a
telescope and then burst open like an
umbrella in an
explosion of
rainbow
colours.
It hung
magically
above
the three
fairies,
sheltering
them from
the hail.

"Let's fly up and look from above," said
Kirsty. "That's our best chance of spotting
anything unusual."

100

Hovering just below the thick, grey clouds, the fairies saw the whole of Goblin Grotto laid out below them like a living map. Smoke was curling out of the little chimneys, goblins were hurrying home through narrow streets, and there was a ragged-looking Christmas tree in the central square.

"Where would Jack Frost hide a pudding?" asked Rachel, gazing around.

"I suppose it might not be here at all," said Kirsty, starting to wonder if her idea had been completely wrong. "Or it could be inside one of the goblin huts."

"We have to keep searching," Elsa insisted.

They zigzagged over the village, trying

to spot the little pudding. It seemed hopeless to think that they could find it in such a dark, grim place. The hail eased off and stopped. It was replaced by a fine, cold drizzle.

"Look!" cried Rachel. "Down there!"

Baker Jack's Just Desserts

They were flying above a patch of frozen ground, where five goblin children were playing catch.

"Look at their ball," said Rachel. "There's something strange about it."

The fairies fluttered closer. From the way the goblin children were throwing the dark ball, it was obviously very heavy.

A bright-green sprig of holly was sticking out of it.

"It's the precious pudding!" Elsa exclaimed in excitement. "Oh my goodness, I hope they don't drop it!"

They zoomed towards the children, just as one of them lunged for the pudding and tripped. The pudding hurtled towards the wall of a house.

"No!" cried Kirsty, diving sideways.

She caught the pudding half a second before it would have hit the wall. Her heart was hammering as she clutched the precious pudding to her chest. She saw Elsa heave a sigh of relief and fly towards her.

"Thank you from the bottom of my heart," Elsa said.

Gently, Kirsty handed the pudding to Elsa. The goblin children had gathered around them, frowning.

"Hey, that's our ball!" one of them squawked. "We found it lying in the snow. Give it back!"

"I'll tell my dad!" another added.

"I don't expect it was a very good ball," said Elsa. "Besides, it belongs to me. But I will give you something much better."

She waved her wand, and a big ball covered in green splodges popped out of nowhere and bounced into the arms of the smallest goblin child. The other children let out high-pitched squeals and then they all ran off to play.

"It's time for us to go," said Elsa with a smile.

Rachel and Kirsty felt Elsa's magic surround them, and then the grey chill of Goblin Grotto disappeared. They were back in the Fairyland Palace kitchen, but it was a very different place from when they had left. Now, the fairy chefs were singing as they whizzed through the air. Cakes were rising, egg whites were stiffening and the kitchen was filled with delicious aromas.

"There's one more thing I must do," said Elsa.

A thin stream of
sparkling fairy dust
curled out of her
wand tip and
filled up the
girls' lockets
once more.

"Thank you,"
said Rachel and
Kirsty together.

"No, *I* should be
thanking *you*," Elsa replied. "Your quick
thinking has saved my precious pudding.
I would never have found it without you.
Now it's time for you to go home, but
I will see you again soon. The gala is
tomorrow, and I am sure that I will need
your help to find the inviting invitation!"

"We'll be ready," Rachel promised.

She and Kirsty waved, and then there
was a dazzling flurry of tiny lights,
as bright and white as snowflakes.
When the lights cleared, the girls found
themselves back at the Christmas Market
in Wetherbury. Once again they were
standing behind Jack Frost's stall, but the
noise of the crowd had died down.

"Come on," said Kirsty, taking Rachel's hand. "Let's go and see what happened here."

The crowd in front of Jack Frost's stall was already breaking up and moving away. A few moments later, all the stalls were busy again, and people were sampling the food and smiling. Mrs Tate waved to the girls as she bit into a mince pie.

"Look," said Rachel, nudging Kirsty.

Jack Frost was glaring at them from inside his stall, and his goblin assistant was sticking out his tongue.

"He must have realised that we found the pudding," said Kirsty.

Jack Frost and the goblin turned and stomped off, and Rachel and Kirsty exchanged a smile.

"Two magical objects found, and one to go," said Rachel. "I hope that we can find the inviting invitation before the gala tomorrow. Jack Frost looks so cross, I'm sure he'll make it as difficult as he can."

"I'm not scared of Jack Frost," said Kirsty. "Together, we're more than a match for him!"

The Inviting
Invitation

Contents

The World Stands Still

"Being outside in the snow is brilliant fun," said Rachel. "I love throwing snowballs and sledging and building snowmen. But the feeling of getting dry and warm afterwards is just as good!"

It was Sunday evening, and the snow had been falling all day. Rachel and Kirsty were sitting by the living room fire toasting their feet, cosy in fluffy dressing gowns and woolly slippers. The lights were out, so everything was bathed in the glow from the fire and the flicker from the candles on the mantelpiece.

The girls sipped their hot chocolate and watched the silent snowflakes tumbling to the ground. Mr Tate walked over to the window and started to draw the curtains.

"Oh, Dad, please will you leave them open for a bit longer?" Kirsty pleaded.

"It makes everything feel extra Christmassy when it snows," added Rachel.

"It just makes me think about all the snow I'll have to shovel tomorrow," said Mr Tate with a laugh. "I could hardly open the front door this morning!"

"We'll help you," Kirsty offered. "And

then perhaps we could build a snowman
in the garden."

She knew that her dad loved building
snowmen, even though he pretended it
was just for children!

Mr Tate grinned, ruffled Kirsty's hair
and went into the kitchen.

"It's been such a lovely day," said Rachel, stretching out her legs and wiggling her toes. "They had the best stalls yet at the Christmas Market."

The girls had spent all day looking around the stalls, and the time had passed in a flash. They had been very surprised when Mrs Tate told them it was time to go home for tea.

"It doesn't matter that the town is snowed in," said Kirsty. "We got all our presents, cards and wrapping paper today, without needing to go anywhere else. The scarf you found for your mum is so pretty."

124

"And your mum will love the handmade candles you bought," Rachel added with a smile.

Kirsty glanced up at the clock. It was almost seven o'clock.

"Elsa said that we would be magically taken to Fairyland at seven o'clock," she said in a whisper. "That's the best thing of all about today – the Royal Gala will be starting soon and we'll be there."

"We'll be guests of honour," said Rachel with a wriggle of excitement.

"It seems a bit strange that we haven't seen Elsa all day," said Kirsty, draining her mug of hot chocolate. "I thought she'd come looking for us when we were at the Christmas Market."

"Maybe she's already found the inviting invitation," Rachel replied.

Before Kirsty could reply, the clock
on the mantelpiece began to strike. On
the seventh chime, everything around
the girls fell still. The snowflakes outside
stopped falling as if someone had frozen
the world, and a passing owl hung
motionless in mid-air. Even the flames
that had been licking upwards in the
fireplace were now as still as a picture.

"Time has stopped," Kirsty whispered.

The girls knew exactly what that
meant – they were off to Fairyland for
the gala! They felt themselves being
lifted gently from the cushions, and as
they rose into the air they shrank to
fairy size. Their delicate wings unfurled,
and their dressing gowns and slippers
disappeared. When they looked down,
they were wearing sparkling party

dresses and glittery
ballerina pumps,
decorated with
tiny silk bows.
There were
matching silk
bows in their
hair, and they
quickly reached out to
take each other's hand.

"Hold on tight!" said Rachel.
"Fairyland Palace, here we come!"

Mysterious Magic

A cloud of glimmering fairy dust puffed out around the girls, and for a moment they could see nothing but sparkles. Then the fairy dust was blown away by a rough gust of wind, and they saw that they were standing on a hill under a starry sky.

"Look, there's the palace," said Rachel, pointing down at the familiar pink towers. "That's odd. I wonder why the magic has brought us here. Shouldn't we be in the ballroom?"

"Perhaps it's because we're guests of honour," said Kirsty, feeling uncertain. "Never mind, it's not far to fly."

Feeling puzzled, but still very excited about the gala, the girls set off towards the palace.  They hadn't gone very far when a huge gust of wind took them by surprise. They went tumbling and somersaulting through the air, in completely the wrong direction.

"Are you all right?" asked Rachel as soon as they were the right way up again. "That was sudden!"

They set off again, but the wind started up at the same time. It was blowing against them as hard as they could flap their wings.

"This is so strange," said Kirsty. "Let's try putting our arms around each other and using our wings together."

They wrapped their arms around each other, but it made no difference at all.

The wind blew stronger and stronger, and however hard they tried to fly towards the palace, they always ended up heading in the opposite direction.

Panting, they fluttered down and sat on the hillside. At once, the wind dropped down.

"There's no point trying again," said Rachel. "It'll start blowing a gale as soon as we fly towards the palace."

"Some sort of magic is keeping us away from the gala," said Kirsty.

"Then perhaps we should use magic ourselves," said Rachel. "The fairy dust in our lockets carried us to Elsa from the human world. Let's see if it'll work the same way here in Fairyland."

Sitting side by side, Rachel and Kirsty opened their lockets at the same time.

"Please lead us to Elsa," they whispered.

Then they blew the dust as if they were blowing out birthday candles after a wish. It scattered at first, but then gathered itself into a shining ribbon that fluttered ahead of them in the opposite direction from the palace.

"Shall we follow it?" asked Kirsty.

"We never say no to adventure!' Rachel exclaimed, zooming into the sky.

The ribbon wound ahead of them, and they followed it easily. No rough winds blew them off course. But gradually the stars disappeared behind clouds and the air grew chillier. By the time they saw a forest ahead of them, the girls were shivering in their thin party dresses. It was an eerie-looking forest, with dark trees that huddled together as if they were scared.

"I know this place," said Kirsty. "It's the forest near Jack Frost's castle. Why is the fairy dust bringing us here?"

"What if it's a trap?" Rachel said, feeling anxious.

They paused and hovered above the

treetops, looking at each other.

"We asked the fairy dust to lead us to Elsa," said Kirsty eventually. "I think we have to trust it. If she's in trouble, she might need us."

"You're right," said Rachel. "And whatever happens, we'll be together."

They flew on, and then the ribbon suddenly plunged downwards and disappeared into the dense forest.

Rachel and Kirsty dived down too, and
found themselves chasing the glittering
ribbon around tightly packed tree trunks.
They flew on faster and faster, until at
last they emerged into a clearing.

The ribbon wrapped itself around a large cage in the middle of the clearing, shone as brightly as a star for a split second, and then vanished in front of their eyes. Rachel and Kirsty gasped in shock. Elsa was trapped inside the cage!

Forest Rescue

In the light of the moon, the girls saw
that Elsa's wand was lying on the ground
near to the cage. Rachel picked it up and
handed it through the bars to Elsa, who
tapped the lock and set herself free.

"Oh, Elsa, what happened?" asked
Kirsty, throwing her arms around her
fairy friend.

"Jack Frost happened," said Elsa in a serious voice. "He set a trap to catch me, and then told his goblins to lock me up in here. That's why I didn't come to fetch you earlier. I've been here since this morning!"

"How did we get transported to Fairyland while you were locked up?" Rachel asked.

"Luckily it was Queen Titania's magic

that brought you here," Elsa explained. "She organised your invitations herself, as you are the guests of honour."

"I'm so glad we were here to help," Kirsty said.

All three friends shared a big hug. Elsa looked as if she wanted to cry, but she took a deep breath and held back her tears.

"I'm scared that Jack Frost has beaten me," she said. "Because the inviting invitation is missing, all the fairy guests will find it impossible to get to the palace.

It's almost time for the gala to begin, and Jack Frost has taken his goblins to the palace so that they can be the only guests and gobble up all the food and drink. I think it's too late to do anything about it."

"It's never too late to stop Jack Frost being mean," said Rachel. "The first thing we have to do is to get to the palace. We'll think of a way to get the invitation back once we're there."

"But how can we get to the palace when the magic is keeping all the guests away?" Kirsty asked. "We tried for ages,

but the wind kept blowing us in the
wrong direction."

"That's it!" Elsa exclaimed. "You
couldn't get near the palace because you
are guests. But what would happen if you
were helping to
organise the
gala?"

She tapped
each of
them lightly
on the head
with her
wand.

"You are
now my personal assistants," she said.
"The organisers don't need invitations to
attend the gala, so hopefully the magic
won't stop you."

"There's only one way to find out," said Rachel. "Come on – there's no time to lose!"

With Elsa in the lead, they flew upwards and soared into the starry sky, flying away from the Ice Castle as fast as they could. The air grew warmer as they neared the palace, but the wind was no more than a light breeze.

At last they landed next to
each other outside
the palace door
and shared
smiles of relief.
Bertram the
frog footman
hurried down
the steps
towards them,
grinning from ear
to ear.

"It worked!" said Kirsty.

"Now we've got a chance," said Elsa.

"Thank goodness you're here!"
Bertram exclaimed. "Not a single
guest has arrived and I have no idea
where the king and queen could be.
The chefs have locked the kitchen doors.

The only ones here are Jack Frost and a
gaggle of goblins!"

"Come on," cried Rachel. "We have to
get to the ballroom and stop them!"

Bertram flung open the door and the
three fairies zoomed down the corridor
to the ballroom, their hearts racing.

Would all the decorations be spoiled and all the food trampled underfoot? What havoc had the naughty goblins created?

Christmas Spirit

Rachel, Kirsty and Elsa burst into the ballroom, worried that everything would be in a mess. But the decorations were still in place and there was no sign that any food had yet been eaten. The goblins and their master were standing around the room with their shoulders hunched and their arms crossed, looking utterly miserable. Jack Frost spotted the fairies and glowered at them.

"This is the worst, most boring, stupid party ever!" he complained. "There's no music, no food and no fun."

"What did you expect?" exclaimed Kirsty. "You've kept all the guests away and locked the main organiser up all day.

Of course it's not much of a party! All the fairies who would make it fun haven't been able to get here because you stole the inviting invitation."

"But I want my own Christmas party!" Jack Frost wailed, stamping his foot. "Tell these nincompoop goblins how to make my party festive!"

"There's only one way that you're going to be able to have a jolly Christmas party," said Rachel. "You have to let the Christmas spirit in and allow *everyone* to have a happy time – not just you!"

"Stop blaming me," Jack Frost grumbled. "It's not my fault!"

"Oh, yes it is," mumbled a goblin in the corner.

Jack Frost shot him an angry look, and then a loud growl echoed around the ballroom. The goblins clutched each other in terror, and even the fairies moved a little closer together.

"Whatever was that?" asked Elsa.

"It was my tummy," Jack Frost snapped. "I'm hungry, all right?"

He scowled at her, and then reached into his pocket and pulled out a piece of shining golden paper.

"The inviting invitation!" Kirsty whispered.

Jack Frost handed it to Elsa, and she gave him her biggest, happiest smile in return. Then something truly magical happened. Jack Frost's mouth twitched and then curved upwards into something that was very nearly a smile.

"I think he really *is* feeling the Christmas spirit!" said Rachel.

Elsa raised her wand and hundreds of mistletoe sprigs appeared, hanging from the ceiling.

"The finishing touch!" said Elsa.

Just then, they heard voices growing
louder by the second. Then a crowd of
fairy guests seemed to explode into the
ballroom, shaking snow from their wings
and party dresses, laughing and calling
out to each other. The Music Fairies took

out their instruments and hurried to take
their places. Magical food and drink
trays floated into the room, carrying
crystal glasses of warm berry juice.
The fairy chefs entered the room in an
elegant line, each carrying a plate piled
high with delicious food. The ballroom
was soon buzzing with conversation and
excitement.

The sound of trumpets made everyone turn, and then King Oberon and Queen Titania swept into the room.

Together with all the fairies, Rachel and Kirsty curtsied.

"Welcome to our Christmas Gala," said Queen Titania. "And a very special welcome to our guests of honour, Rachel and Kirsty. Without them, there would be no gala!"

The fairies burst into a round of applause, and Rachel and Kirsty felt pleased and embarrassed all at the same time. The queen smiled at them.

"You are very welcome in Fairyland, as always," she said. "We have a wonderful evening planned. There will be some exciting performances before the dancing begins. But first I have a little surprise of my own ..."

Goblins, a Gala and a Gift

Queen Titania waved her wand, and suddenly each guest found a little present in his or her hand, wrapped in sparkling gold paper and decorated with ribbons and bows. The goblins jumped up and down in glee, and even Jack Frost had an excited twinkle in his eyes. Rachel and Kirsty smiled at each other and tucked

the presents into their pockets, because
the first performance was about to begin.

The Music Fairies nodded at each
other, and then the first notes of a ballet
solo from *The Nutcracker* echoed

around the
room. Giselle
the Christmas
Ballet Fairy
pirouetted into
the centre of
the ballroom.
The guests
stepped back
to make a
circle around her,
and watched her
beautiful dancing in
delight.

As the applause
for Giselle faded,
Destiny the Pop
Star Fairy stepped
into the circle.
Shaking back her
shining hair, she
launched into a
song that soon had
everyone swaying to
the music. Even King
Oberon was tapping his

foot! At the end of the song, the guests
cheered and clapped, and then Saskia
the Salsa Fairy twirled into the air and
hovered above them.

"Now that Destiny's got you all in the
mood for dancing, it's time to liven this
party up with a group salsa!" she said.

Elsa

"Everyone grab a partner and find a space."

The Music Fairies played a salsa song, and everyone started moving their hips, spinning and copying the moves that Saskia showed them. Rachel and Kirsty faced each other, shimmying to the rhythm and laughing. The king and queen were watching the dance from their thrones, but Jack Frost amazed everyone by asking Elsa to dance!

Trays of drink and food floated through
the dancing crowd, and flashes
of light surrounded
them as Brooke the
Photographer
Fairy flew
above taking
pictures.
Rachel
and Kirsty
danced
until their
feet were
sore, changing
partners every
now and then so
they could dance with
as many of their fairy friends as
possible.

It seemed as if no time at all had passed before the palace clock struck midnight, and the Music Fairies played their last song.

"Merry Christmas!" cried Elsa, fluttering over to hug Rachel and Kirsty. "I thought this Christmas was going to be a disaster, but you two have made it my best Christmas ever. Thank you!"

She hugged them, and all the other
fairies crowded around to wish them a
merry Christmas too. Silver bells tinkled
and the sound of friendly voices rang
in their ears. Then the colours of the
ballroom blurred and shimmered, and the
girls were back in Kirsty's sitting room
in their dressing gowns and slippers. The
snow was falling outside and the flames
were flickering in the hearth.

"No time has passed at all," whispered Kirsty with a happy smile.

"Tell that to my dancing legs!" said Rachel, laughing. "Wasn't it wonderful?"

They shared a hug and then broke apart as something hard came between them. Reaching into their pockets, they each pulled out a little golden package.

"Our presents from the king and queen!" said Kirsty. "I'd forgotten all about them!"

With eager hands they untied the ribbons and opened the crackling paper. Inside they each found a golden hairband with little mistletoe beads hanging from it. They put them in each other's hair and snuggled closer to the fire, feeling sleepy.

"It's been a magical start to Christmas," said Kirsty, leaning against her best friend.

"It has," said Rachel. "And now that Elsa has her magical objects back, everything about this Christmas is going to be absolutely perfect!"

The End

Now it's time for Kirsty and Rachel to help...

Susie the Sister Fairy

Read on for a sneak peek...

The driveway of Golden Trumpet Adventure Camp was packed with cars.

"There's Kirsty," shouted Rachel Walker, jumping up and down as she saw her best friend's car drive up and park.

Kirsty Tate scrambled out of the back and dashed towards Rachel.

"I'm so excited about this week I can't stop thinking about it," said Kirsty as they shared a hug. "I even think about it in my dreams."

"I can confirm that she hasn't talked about anything else for weeks," said Mrs Tate, carrying Kirsty's rucksack over to them. "I'm so glad that we saw the camp advertised in the local newspaper."

"It was a brilliant idea, Mum," said Kirsty.

Rachel and Kirsty hugged each other again. Golden Trumpet Adventure Camp was exactly halfway between their homes in Wetherbury and Tippington. When Mrs Tate had suggested it, the girls had agreed that it was the perfect place to spend some time together.

Looking around, they saw a big wooden building behind them, with a big sign over the door.

Golden Trumpet Adventure Camp
Dining Cabin and Offices

A forest surrounded the dining cabin, and the sound of birdsong filled the air. A young man jogged over to them with a warm smile.

"Hi, I'm Tristan," he said. "I'm one of the camp leaders. It's our job to look after you while you're here and make sure you have a great time."

Rachel and Kirsty introduced themselves and Tristan checked their names on a list.

"You'll be staying in Maple Cabin," he said. "You will be sharing it with two other girls, but they haven't arrived yet. Follow me and I'll take you there."

The girls said goodbye to their parents, picked up their rucksacks and followed Tristan into the leafy forest. The winding trail was so narrow that they had to walk in single file.

"The forest is full of trails like this," Tristan said. "This one is the quickest way from your cabin to the dining cabin."

"What sort of things will we be doing this week?" Rachel asked.

"Too many for me to remember," said Tristan with a grin. "There's horseriding, waterskiing, hide-and-seek, obstacle courses, climbing, cycling – it's going to be great fun. Here we are – welcome to Maple Cabin."

Read Susie the Sister Fairy to find out what adventures are in store for Kirsty and Rachel!

Calling all parents, carers and teachers!
The Rainbow Magic fairies are here to help
your child enter the magical world of reading.
Whatever reading stage they are at, there's
a Rainbow Magic book for everyone!
Here is Lydia the Reading Fairy's guide to
supporting your child's journey at all levels.

Starting Out

1 Our Rainbow Magic Beginner Readers are perfect for first-time readers who are just beginning to develop reading skills and confidence. Approved by teachers, they contain a full range of educational levelling, as well as lively full-colour illustrations.

Developing Readers

2 Rainbow Magic Early Readers contain longer stories and wider vocabulary for building stamina and growing confidence. These are adaptations of our most popular Rainbow Magic stories, specially developed for younger readers in conjunction with an Early Years reading consultant, with full-colour illustrations.

Going Solo

3 The Rainbow Magic chapter books - a mixture of series and one-off specials - contain accessible writing to encourage your child to venture into reading independently. These highly collectible and much-loved magical stories inspire a love of reading to last a lifetime.

www.rainbowmagicbooks.co.uk

"Rainbow Magic got my daughter reading chapter books. Great sparkly covers, cute fairies and traditional stories full of magic that she found impossible to put down" - Mother of Edie (6 years)

"Florence LOVES the Rainbow Magic books. She really enjoys reading now" - Mother of Florence (6 years)

The Rainbow Magic Reading Challenge

Well done, fairy friend – you have completed the book!
This book was worth 10 points.

See how far you have climbed on the
Reading Rainbow opposite.

The more books you read, the more points you will get,
and the closer you will be to becoming a Fairy Princess!

Do you want your own Reading Rainbow?
1. Cut out the coin below
2. Go to the Rainbow Magic website
3. Download and print out your poster
4. Add your coin and climb up the Reading Rainbow!

There's all this and lots more at
www.rainbowmagicbooks.co.uk

You'll find activities, competitions, stories, a special
newsletter and complete profiles of all the
Rainbow Magic fairies. Find a fairy with your name!